Tales On Canglford Nock Volume 1

Written By Tamsin Wood

Illustrated By Sarah Waterfield

This book is dedicated to
My family,
In particular
Master Thistleberry
And
Miss Shimmersprite
who encourage
and inspire me
to believe
every day.
I love you.........xx

Contents

Imogen Shimmersprite's
Search for Happiness

Little Imogen Shimmersprite loved to be kind
and a happier fairy would be hard to find,
She liked catching the sunbeams and rainbows and stars
and she'd give them as presents in tiny glass jars.
If a fairy felt even a little bit sad,
She would give them a reason to smile and be glad,
Even Samuel, the grumpiest fairy would say,
That an "Imogen hug" would make anyone's day.
She would sing happy songs as she watered the flowers
and then talk with the birds and their babies for hours.
She made time just to chat if you needed a friend
and she never did moan or complain or pretend.

Now one day she awoke and she didn't feel right,
For she'd had a peculiar dream in the night.
She had dreamt that a creature hid under her bed,
and stole all of the happy thoughts out of her head.
She got out of her bed and then went to get dressed,
But by breakfast time she felt completely depressed,
For no happy thoughts came to her - not even one,
and big horrid grey clouds had all covered the sun.
All the birds would not sing and the fairies were sad,
Which made Imogen feel inexplicably bad.
She knew something would have to be done and quite fast,
Or all happiness could soon be lost in the past.

Off to see Lola Moonbeam she went straight away
and she told her "I'm having a TERRIBLE day!"
"I cannot find a thing to be happy about
For my mind is just filled up with worry and doubt"
Seeing Imogen look so incredibly sad,
Got Miss Lola upset and a little bit mad.
She decided right then to find Imogen's smile,
So she made them some tea and she thought for a while.
Then at last she stood up and took Imogen's hand,
They flew off through the wood to the edge of the sand.
Far away to the north was an island so small,
You would hardly have known it was out there at all.

On the island was hidden a cave underground,
Where a dragon called Hirador was to be found.
He did not like the fairies or magic or fun,
and lived deep in the shadows and hated the sun.
He spent day after day sitting all on his own,
For without any friends he was always alone.
But today he was feeling a little unwell,
Though what seemed to be wrong he could not really tell.
He had woken up happy and in a good mood,
and he wasn't fed up and he wanted some food.
As the fairies looked up and they saw him they froze,
for he looked rather scary and big, I suppose.

But the dragon just smiled and he asked them to stay
"Oh you mustn't be frightened - please don't fly away!"
"I will show you my cave and then make us some tea,
Won't you wait while I get you a lamp and you'll see".
So he brought them a jar that was bursting with light,
It was Imogen's happiness fastened up tight.
"Well I found this last night when I just couldn't sleep
it was pretty and something I just had to keep"
For it made me feel happy, I used to feel blue,
and it came from a fairy's house .... wasn't it YOU?!"
Then he realised what he had done in a flash,
and felt terribly guilty for being so rash.

For Miss Imogen's happiness had to be shared,
and when Hirador took it he just hadn't cared.
"I'm so sorry I took it I couldn't resist,
and I never imagined that it would be missed.
Now I know you are sad because I was sad too,
Please just tell me whatever it is I must do".
"I need all of it back", little Imogen said,
"Oh I must have my happy thoughts back in my head,
For the reason I share them all out every day,
Is that Love is not Love if not given away".
Now no longer the dragon he had been before,
Poor old Hirador wept as he slumped to the floor.

But then Imogen hugged him and said "Do not cry,
It will all be alright so let's wipe those tears dry.
Now come share all the joy and the good feelings out,
Because that after all is what love's all about,
It is not what you get but what you choose to give,
That defines who you are and the life you will live.
So when somebody does something kind just for you,
Pay it forward and share it – that's what you should do.
Now here's what's going to happen, you'll come live with me,
and then you can share all of my happy for free".
So with Imogen's help mighty Hirador found,
His way into the light from the dark underground.

He moved out of his cave and took up his new post,
Giving all of the fairies what matters the most.
Every day they delivered to every address,
One small jar full to bursting no more and no less.
Each one filled up with joy, love and laughter and fun,
and then topped off with sparkle as bright as the sun.
To this day they continue to make people smile,
Spreading positive thoughts out to every child.
Bringing comfort and warmth to the darkest of days,
They give hope to the helpless in so many ways.
Which means that is the end of the story I guess,
Of Miss Imogen's search for her happiness.

THE END

Hayden Bumblebutt
The Summer Camp Stowaway

Up on Canglford Nock as another day dawned,
Young Reece Beetlebug sat up in bed and he yawned,
Then he put on his slippers and tiptoed next door.
Yes! Today was the day he had long waited for.
At long last he was off on his first summer camp,
He had packed all his kit and then polished his lamp.
His smart uniform hung on the door with his cap,
Whilst laid out on his desk was his compass and map.
He ate up his breakfast before he got dressed,
Tied his boots, and then put on his shirt neatly pressed.
Reece fastened at his tie as he walked to the gate,
Just as all of a sudden a voice shouted "Wait!"
His brother came running to gave him a hug,
"Have great fun and good luck at your camp little bug"
"Take good care of yourself and be safe but have fun,
Do all that you are told and respect everyone".
Reece was quiet for a moment then softly he said,
"Will you be here meet me when it's time for bed?"
"I will see you at sunset – go, be on your way,
Now farewell little brother and have a great day"

But as Reece made his way to the camp rendezvous,
Neither he nor his brother had noticed or knew,
Hayden Bumblebutt quietly sneaking away,
When he should have been doing his chores for the day.
He just wanted to be at the camp even though,
He was not even five and was too young to go.
His big brothers were always the ones having fun,
But now HE was about to show EVERYONE.
That HE was a big boy - of course he was cool,
and he'd get to build tents and go swim in the pool.
He would learn to tie knots and to follow a map,
and then he would get himself a smart tie and cap.
He stayed just out of sight hiding up in a tree,
As poor Connor thought "Where could he possibly be?"
"I've searched high I've looked low and I still cannot find,
Now I think I must surely be losing my mind"
As he puzzled how he would locate the young scamp,
He flew swiftly to look for him down at the camp,
To find old Aron Ferntwig the scout leader who,
being clever and kind, would know just what to do.

As they hunted around all at once Connor saw,
A small boat on the water, quite far from the shore
It was Hayden who'd gone out to fish on the lake,
But he'd lost both his oars - what an awful mistake.
He had found a big dock leaf to use as a sail,
But alas he was drifting alone in a gale.
He clung onto his raft and he cried out in fear,
"Someone help me, I'm stuck and I don't like it here"
Quickly Aron and Connor got into a boat
As their friend Daniel Dragonfly kept them afloat,
Then the fast fairy flyer zipped over the lake,
He left dozens of ripples behind in his wake.
Just as poor Master Bumblebutt started to sink,
Aron pulled him to safety as quick as a wink.
Then the rescue team made their way back to dry land,
Connor gripping on tightly to his brother's hand
Little Hayden was sad for he knew what he'd done,
Had put people at risk and upset everyone.

But his escapade taught him a lesson or two,
and words couldn't express what he already knew.
"Though I promise to never go off all alone,
I just do not like staying at home on my own".
So on Thursday nights after his chores were all done,
Hayden Bumblebutt got to go out and have fun.
He made friends and enjoyed doing sport,
He liked building and once made a huge cardboard fort.
Aron gave him a cap and a belt and a tie,
Plus a badge that was shaped like a small dragonfly,
So each time that he wore it he'd think of that day
and then just to himself he would quietly say.
I am only a young 'un – there's still time to grow.
I have lessons to learn and a long way to go.
It is good to have fun but important for me,
To be honest and kind and act sensibly."
To this day Master Hayden's a well behaved scout,
No more running off hiding or messing about.
Although sometimes he doesn't pick up all his toys,
He is happy for now he is one of the boys.

THE END

Molly MossMuddle's Midsummer Mix-up.

In her red toadstool house on a warm summer's day,
Molly Mossmuddle sang as she tinkered away.
Her entire kitchen table was covered with pans,
lots of packets and boxes, glass bottles and cans.
She had made up a feast for the fairies to eat,
cakes and biscuits and ice cream and other nice treats.
Lots of tiny fruit tarts and some pink lemonade
were already prepared and sat cool in the shade.
In the garden outside all the tables were laid,
wild flowers arranged and some fresh tea was made.
Coloured bunting hung criss-crossed all over the lawn,
fairy lanterns prepared as they partied 'til dawn.
There were big comfy seats and a hammock or two,
lots of button-top stools and a small outdoor loo.
It was going to be an incredible day
there were party games for all the young ones to play.

Lots of Daisy chain making and musical chairs,
then some Lily pad hopscotch and three-legged pairs.
Passing the parcel and leapfrog and tag,
Guess who and a fun game of "what's in the bag?!"
Molly put on her party dress when she was done,
it was time to relax and enjoy all the fun.
Sharp at three was a knock upon Molly's front door,
as the first fairies came followed quickly by more.
Pretty soon all the garden was buzzing with noise,
lots of laughter and chattering fairies with toys.
Miss Molly served food up too busy to see,
Willow Glitternut watching and giggling with glee.
For she'd changed all the tin labels just to confuse
poor Miss Molly who had no idea what she'd used.
Little Willow decided jam sarnies were silly
and she swapped them instead for some hot pickled chilli.

Cakes were sprinkled with pepper and not poppy seeds,
causing all of the fairies to sniff and to sneeze.
As the fairies all spluttered and started to moan,
Willow Glitternut guiltily flew off alone.
What began as great fun had made everyone mad
and now Willow felt lonely, ashamed and quite sad.
As she pondered just how she might possibly fix,
all the mess she had caused with her terrible tricks,
Samuel Thistlefoot found her and said with a frown,
"Do you know that today you let everyone down?"
"The first thing you must do that will make this all right,
is to go straight to Molly to see if she might,
Forgive you for being so naughty and then,
we will see if we can't put things right once again".
Off they flew to find Molly as fast as they could
and found her at last sat alone in the wood.

"I'm so sorry" said Willow "for what I have done
Please, I meant you no harm it was only for fun".
"Now I promise to never play tricks anymore
and I'll help you to make what you tried to before"
"Oh please will you forgive me I'm sorry, I am",
Molly smiled and whispered "Let's go make some jam!"
Once the fairies had eaten they danced and they sung,
and they lit all the lanterns that Molly had hung.
From that day little Willow would always think twice,
About being so naughty and try to be nice.
She never played tricks that made anyone sad
and she tried to be good and not make people mad.
For the motto of fairies is "Help and Be Kind"
and there's no kinder fairy you ever will find,
Than Miss Mossmuddle, baking and cooking all day,
though she keeps all her recipes safe locked away.

THE END

Nathaniel Woodstripe's Workshop of Wonders.

Young Nathaniel Woodstripe kept everything clean,
and no tidier place could you hope to have seen.
He raked up all the leaves and he swept every street,
Up on Canglford Nock so it always looked neat.
Every day he worked hard from sun up to sundown,
and he'd smile even when it was bucketing down.
He would whistle a tune or he'd sing out a song,
So that all of the birds would start tweeting along.
Then as soon as he'd finished his work for the day,
He would babysit fledglings while mum was away.
Then at last when his feathered friends all had been fed,
He would go home for supper and straight to his bed.
Now Nathaniel was shy, not the talkative type,
He preferred to read books and to play on his pipe.
He just loved to invent things from objects he found,
In the trees, on the beach and all over the ground.

But although he was fairly content with his lot,
There was one thing in life that Nathaniel had not,
Was a special best friend to hang out with all day,
Or just talk to if he had a not-so-good day.
One fine day Lacey Cobweb was lazing about,
As the spiders spun webs on the old water spout.
She saw little Nathaniel come out of his shed
and she fluttered towards him quite shyly and said;
"What have you been making – I'd so love to see,
For I bet it's so cool – what on earth can it be?
As he opened the door Lacey tiptoed inside,
and stared totally speechless, her mouth open wide.
For all over the workshop were gadgets he'd made,
Out of rubbish or objects the fairies mislaid,
He'd recycled, invented and built lots of stuff
From the seemingly useless old scraps, bits and fluff.
"That one tells you the weather, this knows how to spell
and the thing on the table plays music as well.

When Miss Lacey said "Please can I ask if I may
But why is it you hide your inventions away?"
Nathaniel looked sad "No one wants to see these
and I'm scared that they'll laugh and tease".
"But these things are amazing Nathaniel you must,
Have some faith in yourself and a sprinkle of trust".
"Oh I can't, I'm the fairy who tidies the place,
I've got dirt on my hands and all over my face".
"That is easily fixed with a lovely hot bath,
I will help you - my house is right there up the path".
Just an hour or so later and all squeaky clean,
He was stood centre stage up on Canglford green.
Well the fairies all listened and watched him with awe,
As he brought his inventions out onto the floor.
They just couldn't believe it and as they all cheered,
Nathaniel's nervousness soon disappeared.

The inventor became the main talk of the Town,
it was teatime before he had chance to sit down.
Then he munched on his dinner and sat for a while,
As they sipped at their tea Lacey said with a smile.
"We had no such idea not one single clue,
You were able to make all our old stuff brand new,
So it was that Nathaniel took up a new post,
Now he spends all his time doing what he loves most.
With a new painted sign hanging over the door,
Master Woodstripe does not need to sweep anymore.
Now with Lacey beside him from morning 'til night,
He spends all day inventing from very first light.
In his "Workshop of Wonders" he made a new start,
All it took was a friend who said "Follow your heart".

THE END

Tamsin Wood/Sarah Waterfield

Published using Createspace.

All illustrations by Sarah Waterfield

ISBN 978 - 1539707004

Printed in Great Britain
by Amazon